ed Red

by Polly Dunbar

Look!
I spy the biscuit jar.
I'll get it down,
It's not *too* far.

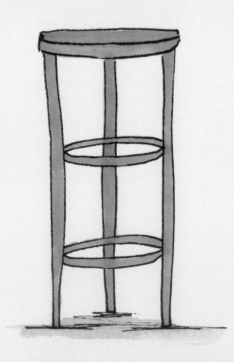

If I just climb ...
stretch ... reach
and jump...

Nearly ... nearly...

"Oh, little one!" says my mum.
"You've banged your head,
that's not much fun."

Yes! I had a bump.
It made me cry.
The biscuit jar
was up too high!

My socks
are
down.

My pants
are
twisted.

I want...

I want...

I WANT

A BISCUIT!

**The lid is on.
And I'm not strong.**

**Everything is
wrong,
wrong,
WRONG!**

Raaah!

I scream.

Graaah!

I roar.

Wump-Wump waa-waa!

I hit the floor.

Watch me while I bang my head!

'Cause now I'm seeing ...

"Oh, Little One," says my mum,
please don't scream,
please don't roar.
It doesn't help to hit the floor.
I know you're seeing
red, red, red,
But why not
count to
10
instead?

"Start with
1
then
2
then
3.
You can do it,
count with me."

2
~~two~~

3
~~three~~

4
four

5
five

6
six

7
seven

8
eight

9

nine

10

ten

And then ...

breathe.

phew-eeeeee.

Look!
My socks are up.

My pants un-twisted.

It must be time
to eat
that biscuit.

A little nibble.
A tiny bite.

Let's see if I can
get this right...

7, 8, 9... WOW!

There's only one
more bite to come
And look, my biscuit is
nom ... nom ...

Gone!

But that's OK.

One more for me, and one for you.
My mum says,
"Ma mwah moo."

And I say ...

"I love you, too."